I0689858

Li Hung-Chang

Celebration of the Seventieth Birthday of Li Hung-Chang

grand secretary, viceroy of Chihli, Imperial commissioner for northern

trade

Li Hung-Chang

Celebration of the Seventieth Birthday of Li Hung-Chang
grand secretary, viceroy of Chihli, Imperial commissioner for northern trade

ISBN/EAN: 9783337118372

Printed in Europe, USA, Canada, Australia, Japan

Cover: Foto ©Raphael Reischuk / pixelio.de

More available books at **www.hansebooks.com**

CELEBRATION

OF THE

◁SEVENTIETH BIRTHDAY▷

OF

LI HUNG-CHANG,

GRAND SECRETARY, VICEROY OF CHIHLI, IMPERIAL COMMISSIONER FOR NORTHERN TRADE.

&c., &c., &c.,

AT

TIENTSIN, FEBRUARY, 1892.

———⟨∞⟩———

TIENTSIN:
THE TIENTSIN PRESS.
MDCCCXCII.

CONTENTS.

THE SEVENTIETH BIRTHDAY OF

THE occasion which brought the Grand Secretary Li Hung-chang into the British Settlement on the 11th February, 1892, to meet the foreign residents in Tientsin, was in all respects a memorable one. The eminent position of the host, especially in connection with the foreign affairs of China ; his venerable age ; his un-failing urbanity to strangers ; his long occupancy of the most important viceroyalty in the empire ; his sympathy with the progressive spirit of the age ; and the liberality of his general policy ; had already earned for the Viceroy Li the respect of all who came in contact with him or who were acquainted with his public life. It needed only such a conjuncture as the Seventieth Birthday, following immediately after his recovery from a serious illness, to impart enthusiasm to the congratulations which were offered to His Excellency on that day.

It is thirty years since Li Hung-chang assumed a conspicuous position in contemporary history. At a time when the Government of China seemed to many observers to be at death-grips with the most formidable rebellion of modern times, Li was appointed to a taotaiship in the province which was then the centre of the movement. The ordinary functions of the territorial officials were of necessity suspended, and their energies devoted to the national defence. It was a time when men of capacity have their opportunity, and the administrative talent of Li Hung-chang soon placed him in a *de facto* position much above his titular rank. The military efforts in Kiangsu had been fitful and ill-arranged when Li was deputed to re-organize the forces which had been raised in and about Shanghai and Sungkiang, the tract of country comprised within the circle of a 30-mile radius round Shanghai being the base of operations against the rebel strongholds which lined the Grand Canal from Hangchow almost to Chinkiang.

It was the distinguishing merit of Li Hung-chang to perceive at a glance the value of that new element of military strength which he found in the Ward force which had been raised in Shanghai; and from his subsequent experience with that force under the leadership of Gordon, to learn the lesson which has been the foundation of his success in life. That lesson was the vital importance of foreign science both to the defence and the material progress of the country, the recognition of which thenceforth became the controlling factor in his public career.

Li had the special good fortune to draw to his standard foreigners of the highest quality, such as Gordon, Macartney, Giquel, and many others; by whose assistance, after the suppression, mainly through their aid, of the rebellion, he was enabled to lay the foundation of those Government factories which have since become so im-

portant. It was at Shanghai and Nanking that foreign
machinery and scientific skill were first seriously employed by the Chinese Government ; and all the Arsenals
in China, at Foochow, Tientsin, and in various places in
the interior, as well as the application of foreign appliances generally, had their origin in the two Arsenals
which were founded or extended under the personal direction of Li Hung-chang.

His successful conduct of the war against the Taiping
rebels, 1862–5, brought honours and promotions thick
upon Li Hung-chang ; it also brought excessive labour.
Recognizing him as the man of the hour, the Government multiplied his functions, loading him with duties so
diverse as almost to require him to be in several places
at once. And such has been his continuous experience
from that day to the present. Made acting, and then full
Governor of Kiangsu in 1862, he acted, in 1863, for
Hsueh-kuan as Imperial Commissioner for Foreign Trade,
and was soon officially appointed to the acting post ; in
1864 he was appointed Examiner for the M.A. degree in
the provinces of Kiangnan. During all this time he was
the active leader and moving spirit in the campaign
against the rebels ; and in 1865 he was made sole Imperial
Commissioner over the troops in Kiangnan. In 1864,
and again in 1865 he was appointed acting Governor-
General of the Liang Kiang, which office he held for two
years, notwithstanding his being a native of Anhui, and
consequently by the settled custom of the Government,
disqualified for the post. As soon as his services could
be spared from Kiangnan he was made Governor-General
of the Hu Kwang, to which office were added, in no
long time, the duties of Governor of Hupei. He was not,

however, destined long to enjoy the comparative ease of
a viceregal Yamên, for on the outbreak of the Nienfei
rebels in Shantung and Honan the task of suppressing
them was entrusted to him. To that campaign he took
with him such following of the foreign adventurers who
had served in Kiangnan as he could collect, but he had
no longer the same choice of men as he had in the former
campaign, and it may also be admitted that his experience
of foreigners was not yet so ripe as to enable him to
exercise an infallible discrimination as regarded the merits
of the candidates for such services. His ultimate success
in quelling the insurrection, after two years of fluctuat-
ing fortunes, was doubtless contributed to by his native
generals more than by his foreign auxiliaries. After a
visit to Peking for Audience towards the end of 1868,
and a short period of retirement, Li Hung-chang returned
to his viceroyalty of Hu Kwang.

But there were still two rebellions on foot: one in
Kueichow and the other in the North-west, both Moham-
medan. In the beginning of 1870 Li Hung-chang was
ordered to take charge of the Government troops in Kueichow, and immediately afterwards, on the failure of Tso
Tsung-tang to subdue the Mohammedans in Shensi, he
was commissioned to lead his forces into that province.
This proved the easiest of all his campaigns, for the
Mohammedans, on hearing of the advance of Li Hung-
chang, promptly evacuated the territory without risking
a single encounter. Before the close of that year Li
Hung-chang was invested with the Governor-Generalship
of Chihli in succession to Tsêng Kuo-fan, in his abnormal-
ly long tenure of which office the traditions of the
imperial service have been made to yield to the paramount

necessity of retaining the most capable Minister of the
Empire in the most important position. To the viceroyalty was added the Imperial Commissonership for
Trade previously held as an independent appointment
by Chunghow ; also that for Coast Defence, and later
the Vice-Presidentship of the Board of Admiralty, Direc-
tor-General of Railways, and other important offices, the
Government apparently considering that no burden could
be too heavy to lay on so broad a back. Added to
these specific duties, which were no sinecure, His Excellency has discharged the highest functions of State in
affairs concerning which he held no definable appointment. He has been the Foreign Minister in all matters
where responsible action was required,—the negotiator
of treaties, the virtual arbiter of war and peace, and
supreme adviser to the Throne.

During these two-and-twenty years that Li Hung-
chang has been conspicuously before the world and in
constant contact with foreigners of all classes, his demeanour and his policy have been entirely consistent
with his previous record, when the name of Li Futai,
the companion-in-arms of Gordon, shone out suddenly
and became a household word on the Coast of China.
One may therefore without much hesitation, and without
waiting for the posthumous revelations which have shed
such a kindly light over the personal character of Tsêng
Kuo-fan, trace the leading motives and the fundamental
aims of one who may surely be set on a higher pedestal,
as a man of action, than even his honoured predecessor.

"Practical" has been the key note of Li Hung-
chang's career. In no depreciatory sense, but in the best
and most patriotic significance of the term, he has been

all his life an Opportunist. Nought of the visionary or the *doctrinaire* in his character has there been to prevent him from economizing to the utmost his energies for such schemes of public utility as were fairly practicable. Hence what he has achieved, in great as well as in small things, has been of durable quality.

Coming into active life at the close of a foreign invasion which exposed the weakness of the empire, and in the midst of a destructive rebellion, the prime need of China appeared to him to be defence; and that, he had the perspicacity to perceive, could only be attained by the annexation of Western science. Although distinguished as a scholar, being a member of the Hanlin Academy, he knew the secret of national security was not to be found in classic lore, but in the inventions and appliances of modern times. And as these could not be introduced into China without the aid of competent foreigners, he engaged them without stint.

The arsenals founded by Li Hung-chang, or organised by him on an efficient basis, is itself an achievement of no mean order. The fleet which last year so impressed that most practical people, the Japanese, that they could not rest until they had taken steps to increase the strength of their own. and the elaborate defences of all the important rivers and estuaries on the Coast. and of the strategical points in the Gulf of Pechili which have cost such immense sums of money. would alone constitute a monument worthy of the greatest statesman. These contributions to the national defence have necessarily been effected in the face of formidable difficulties, for they were all, in the way they were carried out, at variance with national traditions, and required such outlays of money as the Board of Revenue had been wholly unused to.

Neither, however, have the arts of peace been neglected by His Excellency. The creation of the China Merchants fleet was a bold attempt to utilize the resources of foreign science and of business management, in order, by the favour of the Imperial Government, to enrich the Chinese and train them in foreign methods of management. The enterprise cannot be said to have been a failure, although the ineradicable customs of the people have prevented it from realizing all the benefits which it was calculated to confer. The extension of the Telegraph service throughout the empire, long delayed, but pushed forward the moment the circumstances were favourable; the construction of railways whenever and wherever the opposition to them could be overcome; and the encouragement given to mining enterprise everywhere, are all conspicuous examples of that material progress towards which the Viceroy has never for a moment relaxed his efforts. Nor have the results of this policy been restricted to undertakings within his own control, for we see it copied by one of the most influential Governor-Generals in China, one, too, who long bore the character of being the most bigotted anti-foreigner, and who is now an avowed convert to the principles of Li Hung-chang. And like all proselytes, he errs, if at all, on the side of excess of zeal.

In many less obtrusive ways also has the undeviating policy of the Viceroy Li been working towards reform, as in the various teaching establishments he has set up: the Torpedo School; the Military School; the Naval School; the Telegraph School; and the Medical School;

to which may be added, within the last two years, a
Railway School.

In the work of introducing Western science the
Viceroy has stood practically alone. The history, traditions, and the whole dead weight of the national conser-
vatism were against him, a force which the support of his
coadjutors and subordinates was inadequate to counteract.
Indeed, in the retrospect of thirty years of active public
service no feature is more noteworthy than the absence
of those auxiliaries who should have risen to eminence
under so distinguished a leader. The fact comes out as
time goes on with increasing clearness, that what Li
Hung-chang has done, he has, like Coriolanus, done alone,
standing between the halting co-operation of lukewarm
lieutenants unable to seize the wider bearings of his plans,
and the ever-vigilant censorship overhead, readier to
stigmatize failures than to encourage success. In all the
difficulties of an arduous life-service, however, one strong
support has never failed the Solitary Man, the unwaver-
ing loyalty of his Sovereign, to which may be added,
for what it is worth, the appreciation of the civilized
world.

A personage so powerful, not through successful am-
bition, but through having greatness thrust upon him all
his life, might, on a first impression, have been expected
to modify the political atmosphere of his country, and
to make his principles of progress and reform prevail
over the outworn fashions of the public service. But
it is not the work of any single individual, however
influential, to effect radical changes in the ways of a
people. Confucius and Mencius, with all their prestige,
failed when they attempted to reform the administration,

and that too within a very circumscribed area compared with that of the present Chinese empire ; and they had to content themselves with imparting their instructions to a select few, after the manner of philosophers. The man of affairs follows a different method, that of doing whatever lies to his hand diligently and with all his might, thus making tangible contributions to the improvement of the State. For a practical man to expend his vital energy on schemes of general reform would be like shovelling at a mountain of sand while the labour so employed might have been productively bestowed on the cultivation of a given plot of ground. It has been the merit of Li Hung-chang to go with the stream, as far as he could get it to carry him in the desired direction ; but to court no hopeless struggles ; to avoid insuperable obstacles ; and to watch for opportunities. By thus following the dictates of empirical wisdom and common sense he has accomplished something substantial for his country in his own life-time, while the ideal reformer might only have left a name in literature.

So far as personal example can go Li Hung-chang has come out boldly before his own people, above and below him, burst the bonds of convention and braved the reproach of being the friend of foreigners ; has, in fact, swept away the social barriers which hindered the execution of his plans. It is not altogether easy for strangers to realize the degree of moral courage required for any Chinese official to break through established customs and maintain free intercourse with foreigners. The urbanity for which the Viceroy has been throughout his life distinguished, while it has enabled business of all kinds to go smoothly, has materially served the interests of China, an object which His Excellency seems never for a moment to have lost sight of. Free converse with visitors from every corner of the world has been indeed a means of education to the Viceroy in cosmopolitan affairs, and he has unquestionably laid himself out for it with that end in view. These visitors are generally impressed with the pertinence of his interrogatories, and those who come to gain information often end by imparting much more.

The liberal-mindedness of the Viceroy, evidenced by his demeanour towards foreigners, is a quality which has been of the highest consequence in the management of the great affairs of State. The capacity for looking at both sides, the instinct for conciliation, the subordination of the speculative to the practical, have made him the great mediating and moderating force in the foreign relations of China. While in all things upholding the interest and prestige of his country, he would never risk a quarrel on a punctilio, and, bearing always in mind the real proportions of things, would sacrifice the minor to gain the major advantage. He alone, apparently, among Chinese statesmen of the first rank possessing the requisite balance of mind, it is to his hands that all difficult negotiations are entrusted, and even when not directly engaged it is still his counsel that is invoked in emergencies.

Space scarcely admits of even the outlines of illustration of the sagacity and breadth of view which have always marked the diplomatic acts of Li Hung-chang. The time has not indeed yet arrived when the true history of his two principal negotiations with foreign powers can be fully understood. But enough is known to establish his reputation as an able negotiator. In the discussions which preceded the Chefoo Convention of 1876 he had the difficult task to perform of frustrating the demands of his opponent while avoiding the consequences which were threatened; and it is generally conceded that out of a most embarrassing situation he secured advantages to his country which have proved to be of a very substantial character; and by fixing his eye steadfastly on the main object and disregarding trifles, he managed to convert a treaty which was intended to be punitive into an instrument for the aggrandisement of China.

If the negotiations with France between 1883 and 1885 did not result so satisfactorily to China, that was simply because the prudent arrangements of Li Hung-chang were overruled, largely, it may now be said, from personal motives. The Convention first concluded with Monsieur Bourrée would have saved the territory and the subsequent war, but it was refused ratification by the French Government, while it was at the same time condemned by Chinese Chauvinists. It is usually held to be a proof of the equity of a judgment when it gives dissatisfaction to both contending parties. Later, when after their victory at Bacninh, Canton lay at the mercy of the French, and the plans for the capture of that city had been already elaborated with the utmost detail and would have been promptly carried out, Li Hung-chang succeeded in averting that imminent danger by drawing the French into negotiations in the North.

The result was that he concluded with Captain Fournier, on 11th May, 1884, a Convention which, though at once ratified by the Emperor, displeased, once more, the Chauvinists; and influences were brought to bear

in high quarters to prevent the stipulations of the treaty
being carried out.   The peace which the Viceroy had
secured was, at the instance of the malcontents, aided
possibly by suggestions from without, wantonly broken ;
and the year that followed that transaction was perhaps
the most trying in his whole career.   For the personal
feeling of some who stood near the Throne became
involved in the prosecution of a war which could lead
to no satisfactory result for China.   History yet un-
written will vindicate the loyalty, political sagacity, and
the extraordinary self-control which the Viceroy showed
during the whole of that crisis.   But his foresight was
soon justified by the event, for after a year's war,
which cost the country 60 million Taels, and the destruction of the Min fleet, China was glad to accept the
identical terms that Li Hung-chang had previously
obtained, with the 60 millions and the fleet saved.

Emergencies test the realities of things, and nothing
could have so vividly demonstrated the value of the
Viceroy Li to the State than his alarming illness during
the past winter.   On previous occasions he has been
compelled by imperial pressure to forego his family
duties.   The prescribed three years of retirement, while
mourning for his mother, were, after repeated applications,
denied to him, and only with difficulty could he obtain
one hundred days for the performance of the rites.   The
ground for this forcible interference with the pious
ceremonies was declared to be the Viceroy's indispensability.   The same indispensability, which has grown rather
than diminished, weighted the anxiety of the Court and
the public during the few days when the Viceroy was
passing through the crisis of his recent malady ; and it was

the rebound from that anxiety which inspired the feeling of jubilation over the double event of his restoration to health and the occurrence of his Seventieth Birthday.

The serious illness of the Viceroy also severely tested the stability of his own principles. In his weakest moments the pressure of tradition, of the ancient superstitions, the sorceries and soothsayings, and the world of occult influences which haunt the sick-beds of the great, combined with the appeals of affection, to bend his resolution. But he had long since pinned his faith to the true science, the science of things, not of words and dreams, and to no branch of true knowledge had he paid more willing homage than to the medical art. In those trying moments, medical science stood as the representative of all the sciences, and his trusted physician was the representative of medicine. To him therefore, he clung with the confidence of a child, and when the clouds rolled away from the sick-bed it is not difficult to imagine the warm feelings with which the convalescent would greet Dr. Irwin and returning health, feelings which generously overflowed in the complimentary speech made at the grand banquet on 11th February.

It seemed an unhappy coincidence that a quasi-rebellion within his jurisdiction should have broken out at the very time of the Viceroy's illness; but in the event the suppression of the rising has redounded to the credit of himself, his military subordinates, and the rank and file of his troops. The generals proved to be capable, the troops efficient, and though their movements were directed from a sick-bed, their marches were so rapid and well co-ordinated that they accomplished their task in spite of the severity of the cold, from which they

suffered intensely, in the time within which the Viceroy
had undertaken to quell the insurrection. Such a result
was scarcely expected by the majority of onlookers, and
as an evidence of the mobility of the force which has
been organized by him the campaign sheds a lustre
on the name of Li Hung-chang.

The Seventieth Birthday is an occasion of great
rejoicings in any Chinese family; and the attainment of
this age by Li Hung-chang was signalized by the
homage tendered to him by his friends and brother officials in every part of the empire, who vied with each
other in the gifts which they sent, the aggregate value
of which is said to be represented by a very large sum.
His Imperial Majesty crowned all by a choice selection
of precious things, silk, brocades, embroideries, and many
other objects, which were exhibited in a Hall set apart
for the purpose in the Viceroy's Yamên, and were visited
by the whole concourse of officials who came to offer
their congratulations on the New Year and on the
Birthday. Being assured that foreigners also took a deep
interest in the anniversary the Viceroy bethought himself
of a plan by which they might take part in the festivities
proper to the occasion, that the good relations so long
subsisting between the Chinese Authorities and the
Foreign residents might be still further cemented.

THE BANQUET.

The Gordon Hall, the only room capable of receiving
a large company, having been placed at his disposal by
the British Municipality, His Excellency issued invitations
to a banquet to as many as could be seated in the Hall—

about eighty foreigners of all nationalities, of all occupations, and of all positions. The Hall was promptly fitted with a stage and proscenium for the accommodation of the Chinese theatrical troupe who were to perform at the feast; the walls were completely covered with rich embroideries, scrolls and other objects in brilliant colours hung round the Hall, and the vaulted roof was gaily festooned with flags. The effect of the whole was an indescribable harmony which extorted the admiration of every one who entered, and for several days before the feast the decorations attracted a constant stream of Chinese visitors from the city. The credit for this most artistic arrangement is understood to be largely due to the Municipal Surveyor and Secretary, Mr. Bellingham. On the evening of the banquet the whole length of street between the Viceroy's Yamên and the Gordon Hall was illuminated by red Chinese lanterns, the Town Hall itself was brilliantly lighted with gas, while the outside of the building was festooned from the tops of the towers with lanterns, the whole effect being most picturesque and pleasing to the eye.

Punctually at 5 o'clock His Excellency arrived, escorted by his body guard and official suite, and by an immense concourse of people who completely filled the street. He was received at the Hall by Mr. Detring, Chairman of the Municipal Council, by whom the Viceroy was conducted to the ante-room, where he received as many of his guests as could be conveniently presented to him.

On entering the great Hall His Excellency was welcomed with a ringing cheer, and the Town Band played the Grand March composed for H.I.M. the Sultan by

Prof. Terschak. The erect carriage and vigorous ap-
pearance of His Excellency attested his complete restoration to health.

The tables having been arranged so that a Chinese
official of rank should occupy the ends and centre of
each division, the guests seated themselves in the order
shown in the diagram annexed, and the banquet, con-
sisting of alternate Chinese and European dishes, was
served in an admirable manner.

During the repast Mr. Brenan, H.B.M. Consul, proposed the health of His Majesty, the Emperor of China,
which was responded to on the part of H.E. the Viceroy,
by his second son, Li Ching-mai, who in return proposed
the healths of the Sovereigns of the various friendly States.

The toast of the evening was next proposed by Mr.
Brenan in the following words :—

As the one among my colleagues who has been longest in
office in Tientsin, it is my privilege to speak in their name,
and in the name of our respective nationals, in proposing the toast
of the evening. When we consider, gentlemen, the occasion which
H.E. the Viceroy has chosen for inviting us to this banquet, we
not only appreciate the high honour, but we feel ourselves fortunate in
having the opportunity of personally offering to H.E. our congratulations on his attaining his 70th year, and that, gentlemen, attended by
circumstances which must cause H.E. the greatest satisfaction ; for he
finds himself in possession of the complete confidence of his sovereign—
one of the highest positions it is possible to hold—the respect and
admiration of all his countrymen, and a great reputation throughout the
civilised world. If we remember, gentlemen, the unceasing toil which
Chinese official life entails, the many arduous duties H.E. has performed
and the great services he has rendered to the State during the last thirty
years, we rejoice to see him in such robust health, and such mental
vigour and energy as are seldom associated with threescore and ten.
In the course of his long official career, gentlemen, the Viceroy has
served during the reign of four different emperors, and with such zeal,
ability, and unchequered success, that to-day it is face to face with a

statesman who has attained to the very highest position in the official hierarchy that we have the honour to sit. We as foreigners have special cause to congratulate ourselves in finding our lot cast within the limits of H.E.'s jurisdiction, for all foreigners who have occasion to come in contact with the Viceroy, from the Plenipotentiary charged to negotiate an important treaty, to the humble individual occupied with more modest affairs, all have invariably found H.E. ready to extend to them a courteous reception, and to give their requests and representations a patient and reasonable consideration. I will not go so far, gentlemen, as to say that everyone leaves the Viceregal *yamên* entirely satisfied with the result of his interview. To give satisfaction to everybody is not within the power of any man, and H.E. has doubtless often had to bear in mind the words of Mencius, who says: "If a Governor will try to please everybody, he will find the days not sufficient for his work." What the work is in the case of the Viceroy but few of us have any conception. Each of the high posts which H.E. fills, as Viceroy of the province, as Imperial Commissioner for Northern Trade, as Imperial Commissioner for Northern Defences, and as Director of the Naval Board—every one of these high offices implies such an amount of attention and anxiety that we are left to marvel how all this work can be done, and done with such conspicuous success by our illustrious host, who can yet find time to come into our midst and entertain us in this sumptuous manner, and thus give one more proof of the friendly feelings by which he is animated. It is our sincere wish that our noble host may long be spared to give his valuable services to his country. May he long enjoy the favour of his sovereign; may his great reputation still grow greater; and in the future may his sons and grandsons have as brilliant careers as their distinguished sire! Gentlemen, I invite you to drink to the health of H.E. the Viceroy!

The toast having first been delivered in Chinese and subsequently in English, and been drunk by the company with enthusiasm, Mr. Li Ching-mai replied for the Viceroy as follows :—

My father wishes me to reply for him to the words just spoken in recognition of his services to the Emperor and people of China, and to the foreign nations who have wished to be friendly with us on the basis of mutual regard and fairness. Above all, I am to thank you, gentlemen, for the hearty approval with which you have received the sentiments expressed by Mr. Brenan. My father is very happy indeed to be among you, because he likes to show his friendly feeling towards all

classes of foreigners represented to-night under this roof. He
appreciates the interest you have taken in the celebration of
his 7oth birthday, and especially thanks you for your sympathy in the
serious illness through which he has just passed. Accepting your
congratulations and kind wishes for his long life and good health,
my father takes this opportunity to pay a public tribute to western
medical science, to which he owes his presence among you. I am
to couple this expression of the Viceroy's feeling with the name of
Dr. Irwin. To his skill, care, and patience my father, my family, and
our friends are deeply indebted. In my father's name, I call upon
you, gentlemen, to lift your glasses and drink in honour of Dr. Irwin,
his colleagues, and their noble profession.

Towards the close of the repast the theatrical troupe
were introduced and performed several comedies of which
explanations in English were circulated among the guests.
The tables were then dismantled and the hall re-arranged
with the chairs in rows for the audience to witness the
various entertainments which were given them on the
stage, H.E. the Viceroy taking his seat in the middle of
the guests. The fact that the banquet had nothing of
an official or commercial character about it put host and
guests equally at their ease, and there was a sincerity
in the congratulations offered and a heartiness about the
whole entertainment such as is rarely seen on occasions
when host and guests are of different nationalities.

The party broke up about ten o'clock, when the
Viceroy with his official *suite* left the Hall. A dense
but very orderly crowd almost blocked the main
thoroughfare of Victoria Road.

The Viceroy was highly pleased with the ovation he
received; and when he heard of the great admiration
which had been expressed of the rich and beautiful things
he had lent to decorate the Hall he generously presented
the whole to the Municipality as a souvenir of the happy
occasion.

To Earl Li on Reaching the Age of Three Score Years and Ten.

Translated by

C. H. BREWITT-TAYLOR.

During the eighteen years of His Majesty's reign the influence of your councils has been perceptible in every act of state, and your position is now firmly established as first among statesmen. Surely you are He that Hofei was destined to bring forth! Councillor, Governor-General of the Metroplitan Province, Naval Minister, Superintendent of Trade; we see you engaged in these quadruple duties, and in each *facile princeps*. You have vindicated your right to all your titles. Our Prince is indeed fortunate in the possession of such a Minister.

This year on the fifth day of the first month you enter upon your eighth decade, and His Majesty, regarding your welfare as bound up with his own, has honoured you as befitted your age and rank, bestowing on you his autograph and precious jewels, even as of old Kung Kuan received a staff to support his faltering steps and Yang Piao the crown of wisdom. You have held office under four Emperors, and restored a dynasty of which the fate

hung trembling in the balance. By common consent you
are acclaimed worthy of such tokens of respect and of these
high honours. The inhabitants of this great empire seek
good words in which to felicitate you. Your family has
indeed become illustrious, and songs and choruses in its
eulogy resound through the land; the ear is ever hearing,
the hand tires of writing your praises. Why need I then
repeat them ?

I indeed regard our Sovereign as the Illuminant of
the Universe, the brawny-shouldered Atlas, the Ruler
Superior to the famous Nine, the Nourisher of Creation.
His ennobling influence spreads afar, even into the realms
of fancy. In Corea dwell our envoys and Verbiest was
one of our courtiers; Tu Li-ch'ên's mission reached the
Siberian hills and the Ghoorkas came from the confines of
the south. Our influence extends from the land of horses
to the domains of the Lord of the White Elephant; even the
regions where the reindeer and dog are pressed, as beasts
of burden, into man's service are not beyond it. Men of
all nations fly to our shores yearning to wear our dress and
win distinction in our service. Broad is the land, yet those
on its borders are not beyond the fatherly sway of our
Emperor.

Of old, golden vessels came to Ts'in; and the woollen-
clad ones had intercourse with Han. The envoys of Rome
came to us while the T'angs ruled, and under the Yuan
dynasty Chu Ch'ang-ch'un (Fa Hsien) travelled toward
the west. The records of these events are not very complete,
and we can only glean scant particulars from casual notes
and glosses, and from the itineraries of a few ambassadors.
The very name of the Loo-choo Islands is doubtful. It
has been left to Our Dynasty to establish the fixed points to

which all the others may be referred. Harmony now prevails
among the peoples of the earth, and congratulations are
exchanged in many tongues. The demons of To-su trouble
us no more. Foreign treasures in the form of taxes and
tribute flow into our land, while the art of building the
ships that convey them has been stolen from us. These
outside men, however, have developed along their own lines
and they have various literatures among them, as Sanskrit
and its off-shoot Latin, in which successive moral codes
have been written culminating in the Mosaic Decalogue.
Their multi-coloured flags be-deck the seas and their coined
money, bearing the effigies of various princes, abounds
in commerce. Our land has dealt with them in its
righteousness, correcting the faithless and treating true
friends with kindness. Further, we have exchanged
solemn treaties and Royal Messengers.

When our country was troubled within and threatened
without we had indeed such trusty and able councillors,
as Hu Wên-chung[1], Tsêng Wên-chêng[2], and Tso Wên-
chiang[3], yet our griefs were not entirely removed. They
knew well how to repair the house against the threatening
tempest, but internal troubles left no time for external defence. They indeed knew, but could not act; their measures
were incomplete. It was left to You to finish their task.
You restored the Empire and secured our Sovereign Lord.
Far seeing, cautious in action, careful in plans, you
preserved the Son of Heaven. Your genius devised schemes
and worked out details : nothing is too trivial for the
sage's notice. Kuan Chung advised his master; to him

---

1. Hu Lin-i.
2. Tsêng Kuo-fan.
3. Tso Chung T'ang.

the future was an open book ; Tzu Ch'an's generation was
the better that he had lived. Your name is in men's
mouths as was Chou Yen's of old, and you have managed
foreign affairs like Hua Yi. Men from afar have come to
be our neighbours; you have treated them as the Great
Teacher advised, and like Ch'êng Kan you know their
dwelling places. You are altogether admirable, in literature deep, in war-craft terrible, in perception acute, in
genius sublime, you are entrenched on every side, unas-
sailable.

The Odes say :
" Let us cherish this centre of the kingdom." *

and again :
" He will keep all these countries in order." *

and it is written in the Yi-king :
" They carried through the necessarily occurring changes, so that
the people did (what was required of them) without being wearied. Yea,
they exerted such a spirit like transformation that the people felt
constrained to approve their (ordinances) as right." *

You quelled the Taiping rebels and earned your title
of Minister of the North and South. For twenty years you
have faultlessly conducted foreign relations, so that we
shall surely enjoy peace for evermore. Thus I add my
feeble testimony to history.

The Tanguts succumbed to force alone. Political
prescience is the safeguard against misfortunes. The
wrangling border tribes used to infest the roads on our
west; like fishes leaping the waves came the barks of the
eastern sailors. In the reigns of Tao Kuang and Hsien
Fêng heaven glowed in anger, and our leaders showed

---

* Legge's Translations.

their prowess. In our righteousness we struck, but we did not destroy. In truth we were at a disadvantage in weapons and we did not proceed to extremes nor fill the land with tombs.

Ch'ih Yu was the first who fashioned lethal weapons, and Hsüan, though victorious over him, failed to destroy them. Arrows used to reach us from the Amoor, shafts of wood and flint heads. The Chous did not despise the good swords from Tsan Lu, nor did the kings of Ts'in value them lightly. The knives of the Turfans, of temper to cut jade, were esteemed by Mu Tan above jewels. We know of bows shooting multiple arrows, of the cross-bow and the ballista, speedily surpassed by the thunderous fire. The Franks first used the marvellous cannon at Hsi-ching. After the days of the Mings, these reached us from the south. In the charge of P'an Kêng we read: "Get rid of obsolete weapons, seek new." And again in Jang Tsu's book: "Let the spearmen cover the billmen." We have long had these instructions, and You have now taught our armies to use breech-loading cannon and magazine rifles.

Of old the talent of Ch'u was employed in the service of Ch'in, and the weapons of Yüeh rescued Wu. Cordially assisting each other all are benefitted, while quarrels close markets and restrict intercourse. Each country has its own sharp weapons and each thing its uses which may be learned. Did it behove us to stand idly by dependent upon others? Though by Heaven's favour no land is more gifted than ours, yet other races may be more ingenious, even to the verge of being dangerous, and we, in these days, must observe and deduce. All things have a *tao* of construction, and facility is only developed by practice. Chang Hêng was a marvellous inventor, Li Yeh wrote a treatise on geodesy. In our day we see various new manufactures and new arts. We see tools as gigantic in their way as an ox-seething cauldron, as microscopic as if designed to carve a peach stone. Now we see you engaged in strange combinations of elemental vapours, anon measuring the courses of the stars. Control of enormous masses is perfect; delicate measures are made more accurate than the eye can perceive. Machines are constructed of parts numerous as the stars, which, when fitted together, do not permit a grain of corn to pass between their surfaces. To manufacture bows and spears is easy; to use them fittingly, difficult. You established workshops and factories that weapons might not fail us. You have built walls in the face of difficulties stern as those of Wei's when the recalcitrant sand could only be frozen together, and as firm as those of Tung Wang who steamed the clay. Your prescience has fortified vulnerable points; for us earth supplies material, heaven workmanship. Krupp guns protect every river, masked batteries lurk in unsuspected spots, one fort supports another, hills are cut through, towers are raised, soldiers hide within the walls, secret passages provide exit. Possible enemies circle round us even as the Great Bear round the Polar Star; right and left we face as the changing moon. Let enemies advance, you are protected on every side. The very winds favour you; you are able to dive into the depths, or wing your way to the skies. The submission of *three* cities was commemorated by the Yi-ching Tower, but what are three to You? Every port is guarded by impregnable fortresses. To place us on a par with other nations, You established modern schools and secured the services of experienced

technical instructors, so that now "flying clouds" range the
ocean urged by submerged wheels. They ride on the whirl-
wind and laugh at the storm. Canoes and coracles served
our earlier needs, but they are useless against the thunder
and lightning of modern warfare; opposed to our latter-day
ships, they would be crushed like eggs. Seven-fold armour
is not comparable with our steel, which even the ten-fold
sun could not melt. In motion they are under perfect
control; at rest they are as firm as a solid wall.
Their batteries are thunder, their lights vie with the sun
and moon. The leviathans advance heedless of the rolling
waves; swift are they in their course able to carry thou-
sands of men; yet we think them too small! These ships
despise the breath of the mirage-breathing monster, and he
retires, not they. Li Pin fought the supernatural with
like arts: Li Tui-yu's vessels chased away the forest
sprites. A journey to K'un-shên is now a mere excursion,
and You procured for us these immense ships.

The deeds of antiquity may be read, and one may
learn even to slaughter dragons. Li Kuang, the "flying
General," did not confine himself to ordinary methods of
warfare. Weapons and strategy were changed at Ching,
and the Kao vase has yet a significance. Kou Chien
devoted great attention to his naval force, and his armies
were composed of veterans; their training was on the plans
of Pao and Yü. Chariots were drawn up at Yen Ling.
The wise man examines all systems of strategy. The
men of the west are used to warfare: it is to them as
ploughing and sowing. They spend untold treasure in
their military establishments, and devote seven years to
the training of a common soldier. They have field guns
and floating batteries; they have their own systems,

cumbersome, perhaps, and slow in advance and retreat. They devote much time to military science, studying by means of sketches and plans. They take mechanics into the field as well as fighting men. They arrange for one corps to support another just as in our books. We know that Cheng Tzŭ used to admire the discipline of the bonzes, which was based upon that of the ancients : and that Hsiian enquired into the means used by barbarian chiefs to maintain their authority. Aliens have frequently been appointed to office, and armies have succeeded through purchasing the secrets of victory, as when Wu Chien introduced chariot fighting into our army of old. In our days we use fire in various forms, and not least is the modern torpedo, dashing over and through the waves, able to pierce the strongest armour. And You established schools for our instruction in these matters.

Thunder is produced by strife between the two essential elements, and the shock of collision between the Yin and the Wang produces lightning. The Bamboo Books state, though erroneously, that a flash of lightning playing through the Great Bear was the cause of the birth of the first Emperor, and the Record of the Supernatural says that thunder is the sound of laughter of the gods at play. In " T'ang Ch'uan " lightning is the essential heat become visible ; in Chung Yuan it is condensed sunlight. But we use electricity now to convey sympathy in manner more marvellous than the Lo bell's answering to the riven T'ung Hill and quicker than Têng Liu's pursuit of Helion. Like the strings of a mammoth monochord, like an Imperial marking line, the wires edge the roads, stretching from pole to pole. With amazing swiftness to and fro fly messages in the language of those who write on parchment.

Tzŭ Ching tore off a part of his dress to write upon ; but we have no need of migrating swallows. Chii Yuan would now need no pigeons to mobilise his troops. Lan Tzu's dictum that the world could be known to him without moving from his study, and Sakyamuni's that he could circle the globe in a moment are now realized. The King's orders are given direct to his Ministers ; the Court extends to Po-ti. We sit and await news of victory ! nay, battles are fought and won in our very presence. The bounds of our perceptions are unlimited. And the Telegraph System, by which this is secured, is Yours in design and execution.

Yü fed the teeming people and taught them to barter. Li, Feudal Prince of Yüeh, wrote a treatise on trade. The people of Ch'i were fishers and miners. The T'angs used waterways. "Guard our possessions, strive to increase," should be our motto. In the old days Roman ships came hither, and Persian merchants were met in Tang's capital. " Nibble away at the husk and you will at last reach the grain "—this was the guiding principle of the foreigners who came across the seas and entered our ports. We admitted them and they were guests. Presently the positions were reversed: we were guests and they masters. Wishing to stop the drain we had to turn to ourselves for aid. The Wu rice comes from the south, hemp from Shuh, in the west. We saw how we could turn the sea to our advantage and have ships for defence. Now our ships carry the skins of Ch'ëng to the markets of Chow. Produce of every kind pours into every land, and foreign cloth and gold are piled in heaps in our provincial stores. There is plenty for all and poverty ceases to exist. We hold our own and more—" the water begins to return from the sea." These advantages are due to You, for the formation of the Steamship Company was Your work.

At the present day one might believe the empyrean a furnace, and the Yin and Yang fuel. Fire is necessary to cast metals and bake pottery. What should we do without our iron ploughs and cooking-pots? When we neglected our coal it was as sand and mud: now it has become precious as our daily food. Tung Fan discovered what were thought to be the ashes of old-time fires. Su-shih (Su Tung-po) sent in a memorial relating to the smelting of iron. Now we dig deep into the lowest fountains, and only the basic stone of the solid earth stops us. We penetrate into the nethermost hell, and the deep-down caves of the winds. We erect strong machinery and pump up rivers of water needing bridges like the rainbow arch. The valleys of the earth are not large enough to serve as store-houses. Æolus fans our fires. The icy north defied our piles of firewood, but now the boundless stores of fuel dug from the earth renders us proof against the chills of heaven. Chuang Tzŭ's fuel never ceases to glow; Yü Hsü's camp fires might be still more numerous. Ice and snow may cover the earth; we need not call upon the blower of the *lü* to warm our valleys; smoke streams from every chimney, yet we do not laboriously gather firewood. The forge and the fierce furnace never cease to glow. And You opened the K'aip'ing Collieries and laid bare its wealth.

In the words of Ku Liang, "The distant is dim and indistinct." Ying Ping knew that personal acquaintance was worth more than endless questionings. If we wish to impose our ways on the north and south, and influence the east and west, we need the gift of many-tongued

Chu Yü. Yang Chuan's travels in pursuit of Buddhist literature furnished us with some ethnological and topographical knowledge. But as travellers have been few, speculation has supplied the lack of observation, and false notions are manifold. Verbiest's geographical works are far from accurate, and the Western Directory gives but scanty information. The best of these older books are but rough approximations to the truth, and they are by no means exhaustive. However, recently, we have had Wei's maps and newer geographies; we have translations of astronomical and scientific works: we have accounts of the manners and customs of various peoples, the rise and fall of nations, discoveries and inventions: we have all these translated from the most reliable foreign books by the Translation Department organized by You.

The Chous distinguished contracts by the use of red, and the Duke of Ts'in swore by the clear water. Our treaties, with conditions of various kinds, have been made with many nations. At one time the King's commands were conveyed by special envoys, at another the Feudal Dukes met in assembly. At one time a jade *pi* was given as security for territory, at another a vase was the witness of a contract. The Tu-fans raised a stone tablet with conditions sculptured in three styles of writing. By our treaties we have opened ports and granted concessions, to which foreigners flock like busy ants. Yet demand follows demand. Before the oath-blood is dry upon their lips the contract is broken and the pledged jewel threatened with destruction. Now they quarrel with each other, now pledge friendship in deep cups. Precedence, or perchance the meaning of a word, has been excuse enough for a quarrel. But now our

envoys are sent, and theirs received, and peace reigns.
The arrangement of these many treaties is also Your
work.

Good ship timber used to grow in Chou, and Kao's
marine forces were famous. The Hans had a training lake
at K'un Ming, and at Hsi-tu was the first naval fight.
Our naval forces won the day at Lo Lang and Po Hsieh.
The tattooed barbarians used to guard our frontier.
Our capital is our chief care, and our ablest strategist
can in no better way turn his talent to account. Our
ships visit far-off lands, and keep enemies from our shores.
Wei Chiao's people never see the rolling signal fires ; and
the garrison at Pi-tao have nothing to do. Shan-hai-kuan
is within the lines, and Chefoo is securely guarded by
the torpedoes of Wei-hai-wei. The control of these matters rests with Board of Admiralty, which was instituted
on Your advice.

In the old days the Annam envoys pursued their
route by the compass, while the sounding drum recorded
the miles traversed. The sage-like Chou and Hsieh Tu
could not boast of their own handwork, so our records of
these contrivances are scanty. We only know they
existed and were effectual. The flying chariot of Ch'i
Hung and Hu's miraculous shortenings of distances ;—
what know we of these beyond that there were such things?
As Tien Fan, the destroyer, seated in his armoured chariot
passed over the face of the earth, so now, on branching and
interlacing ways, the snorting iron devils, whose breath is
lightning and sighs thunder, tears from place to place
beating down hills and filling valleys that perchance
might impede his course. No latter-day K'ung Ming
would be content with "running horses and wooden oxen."

Our most famous chargers cannot be compared in speed with our railway carriages. In a moment of time we reach the capital from the uttermost parts of the earth. Troops, may be, are needed, and in one day they move from the land of sunrise to the hills of the setting sun, supplies follow as if on wings, and generals seem to drop from the sky. The King's way must be peace, rebellion can no more raise its head—and we have attained this by means of the Railways, which You introduced.

All these great deeds, engaging all the arts and sciences, benefit all peoples and all ages, and urge our people to greater efforts in competition with their foreign neighbours. You, as did the sages of old, unite in yourself all talents, and, as they, are worthy of the tiger's skin and sounding bells. Some have conciliated the barbarians that they may serve as guards to keep out others; some have closed our doors against all-comers; some, having made peace in a district, have taken the credit of pacifying the world; some have applied Nestorian wisdom to explain the gambols of a calf. How they differ, the narrow and the wide, the small and the great! As I stand beside you in the Han-lin I feel how small I am, how little able to grapple with the great matters met with in my province on the great commercial highway. In You we have perfect confidence, and I earnestly desire to learn from You. Compared with You, I am as a simple peasant to a picked archer; a poor jade to a fleet racer. You are men's ideal. You, like K'ang Hou, enjoy the confidence of our Sovereign; Yours is the glory of Chang the Councillor. You are the cynosure of all eyes. By common consent, at once the record and reward of service, is the inscribed vase.

Chang Chih-tung,
Governor-General of Hunan and Hupei,
the author of the above address, and
T'an Chi-hsün,
Governor, the writer,

with:

K'ung Hsiang-lin,
Wang Chih-ch'un,
Ch'ên Pao-ch'ên,
Yün Tsu-i,
Ch'ü T'ing-shao,
K'ung Ch'ing-fu,
Fan Kung-chao,
Chu Ch'i-hsüan,
Hsi Chang,
Ch'ên Ju-fan,
T'sao Nan-ying,
P'êng Shih-hua,
Wang Hsi-hsiang,
Kung Chao,
Chiang Liu-jui,
Yeh Han-chang,
Li Chia-lan,
Ts'ai Hsi-yung,
Chao Pin-yen,
Liu Pao-lin,
Ch'ên Chan-ao,
Li Fang-yü,
Shên Pao-hsiang,
Shih Shu-ch'ing,
Wang I-ch'ing,

Hsü Yu-lin,
Wang Yuan-ch'ing,
Ch'un Hou,
Shu Hui,
F'êng Yün-ku,
Ngö-le-hêng-ngö,
Yen Tsu-ch'ang,
Chih K'o-ch'üan,
Ch'en Kuei-lin,
our colleagues, offer sincere congratulations.

www.ingramcontent.com/pod-product-compliance
Lightning Source LLC
Chambersburg PA
CBHW061239260626
47172CB00003B/927